Hermie

God Listens When I Pray

MAX LUCADO's

Story by **Karen Hill**

Illustrated by **Daniel Howarth**

Tommy NELSON

A Division of Thomas Nelson Publishers

NASHVILLE   DALLAS   MEXICO CITY   RIO DE JANEIRO

Karen Hill, Executive Editor for Max Lucado.

Illustrated by Daniel Howarth.

Published in Nashville, Tennessee, by Tommy Nelson. Tommy Nelson is a registered trademark of Thomas Nelson, Inc.

Tommy Nelson, Inc., titles may be purchased in bulk for educational, business, fund-raising, or sales promotional use. For information, please e-mail SpecialMarkets@ThomasNelson.com.

ISBN-13: 978-1-4003-1748-6

Library of Congress Cataloging-in-Publication Data

Lucado, Max.
  God listens when I pray / by Max Lucado ; illustrated by Daniel Howarth.
    p. cm.
  Summary: Hermie the caterpillar and his garden friends are reminded that God always listens and always helps His children.
  ISBN 978-1-4003-1748-6 (hardcover)
  [1. Prayer—Fiction. 2. Christian life—Fiction. 3. Caterpillars—Fiction. 4. Insects—Fiction.]
I. Howarth, Daniel, ill. II. Title.
PZ7.L9684Go 2012
[E]—dc23   2011026610

Printed in China

12 13 14 15 16 RRD 6 5 4 3 2 1

It was a pretty day in the garden. The sun was shining. All of the garden bugs were busy.

And Hermie? Hermie was *rushing*. He could hardly wait to get to Grannypillar's house. She was making his favorite mint leaf lemonade!

Hermie scooted along the path. He passed his friends along the way.

"Hi, Flo!"

"See ya, Lucy!"

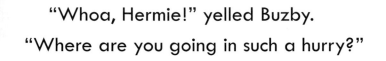

"Whoa, Hermie!" yelled Buzby.
"Where are you going in such a hurry?"

Hermie smiled. "I'm on my way to Grannypillar's house. She is making my favorite mint leaf lemonade! Yum!"

And off he raced again, thinking of the cold, sweet, and sour taste.

Hermie ran around the corner. Then he zipped down the hill and . . . stopped. His buddy Antonio the Ant was kneeling in the middle of the path. His foot was stuck under a big rock.

"Hermie! Thank goodness you are here. Help me!" Antonio said.

"What happened, Antonio?" asked Hermie.

"This big rock was blocking the path," said Antonio. "I was trying to move it out of the way. But it rolled on my foot. Owwww! It hurts!"

Hermie pushed and shoved the big rock. But it would not move. "I'll go get help!" Hermie told his friend.

Hermie ran to Wormie's house as fast as his eight little legs would carry him.

Wormie was resting in his hammock.
He was reading *Super Worm Magazine*.

"Wormie, get up! Something awful has happened! I need help," said Hermie.

"Shhhh . . . ," Wormie said. "I am just getting to the good part."

"But this is important!" said Hermie.

"Uh-huh." Wormie turned the page.

Hermie gave up and ran next door. Maybe Grannypillar could help.

Grannypillar was making mint leaf
lemonade when Hermie rushed in.

"Hermie, you are just in time to go pick
some berries for lunch," she said. Then she
handed Hermie a berry basket.

"Granny, something awful happened! I need you to listen . . ."

But Grannypillar was not listening. She was too busy.

"Run along now and find those berries. I will make you a *berry* sweet pie," laughed Grannypillar. "Tee-hee, *berry* sweet . . ."

"This is no time to think about eating," Hermie said to himself. "I have to find help for Antonio!"

So Hermie went to look for his other friends. But no one had time to listen.

Lucy was teaching Hailey and Bailey how to swim. "Later, Hermie!" she called from the pond.

Just then Hermie heard a familiar and gentle voice. "Hermie. It's Me. God."

Hermie stopped. "Yes, God. I'm here. And excuse me, but I'm in a hurry. I need to find someone to help my friend. He is in trouble, and I can't get anyone to help. They will not even listen to me."

"Hermie."

"Yes?"

"I am listening. I have been listening all day. You have been running all over the garden asking others to help you. But you did not ask Me," God said.

"Oh," said Hermie. "I guess I . . . I sort of forgot."

"That's okay, Hermie. Just remember, I always listen when you pray."

"God, thank You. I feel better already! But my friend Antonio needs Your help. He got his foot stuck under a big rock. Now he can't get out. His foot is hurting. I'm not strong enough to move the rock. And I can't find anyone to help."

Hermie bowed his head, folded his hands, and softly prayed, "Dear God, will You please help my friend?"

"I am proud of you for caring about your friend," God said. "When you need help, pray to Me. I care about Antonio too. I will help him."

"Thank You for listening to me, God!" said Hermie. He hurried back to Antonio.

"Antonio, I am here with you. Let's pray together," Hermie said.

And so they did. The caterpillar and the ant prayed for God to help Antonio. As they prayed, big round raindrops started to fall.

Hermie took a leaf and made a little cup. He filled it with rainwater for Antonio to drink.

"That tastes good," Antonio said. "You are one of my best friends, Hermie."

"Your friends! That's it!" Hermie jumped up. "I will find your ant friends. They can move anything!"

"Good idea, Hermie. They are working over at the anthill."

Hermie told the ants about Antonio. They all ran to help. But when they got there, they were surprised to see that Antonio was already free.

"What happened? How did you get your foot out from under that big rock?" they asked.

"It was the rain!" said Antonio. "The rain made the path soft. So I was able to pull my foot out."

Hermie knew why the rain had come at just the right time. God sent it because they had asked Him for help.

Hermie prayed quietly, "Thank You, God, for sending the rain. You helped my friend."

"Hooray!" The ants cheered so loudly that everyone in the garden came running to see what had happened.